DANGEROUS ROMANCE
COLORING BOOK

ABOUT THIS COLORING BOOK

Explore the very best dangerous romance in this breathtaking adult coloring book! **SIXTY** original and creative illustrations honor the darkest heroes and twisty books we love. Includes exclusive designs for Anna Zaires, T.M. Frazier, Skye Warren, LJ Shen, Laurelin Paige, BB Easton, Willow Winters, R.K. Lilley, Aleatha Romig, and more.

Relax between reading your favorite books with soothing coloring. This coloring book is a MUST HAVE for the shelf of any dangerous romance reader. There are even a few book-themed word puzzles!

COMPLETE LIST OF AUTHORS INCLUDED: Giana Darling, Celia Aaron, Marni Mann, Nikki Sloane, Laurelin Paige, Trisha Wolfe, Aleatha Romig, T.M. Frazier, Claire Contreras, Autumn Jones Lake, M. Never, Anna Zaires, Parker S. Huntington, BB Easton, Tessa Bailey, Stylo Fantome, LJ Shen, R.K. Lilley, B.B. Reid, Natasha Knight, Alta Hensley, Annika Martin, Tara Sue Me, Sierra Simone, Willow Winters, A. Zavarelli, Annabel Joseph, Shanora Williams, Pam Godwin, Tamsen Parker, Pepper Winters, Skye Warren.

TABLE OF CONTENTS

DANGEROUS ROMANCE

COLORING BOOK

TWIST ME ANNA ZAIRES

KIDNAPPED. TAKEN TO A PRIVATE ISLAND.

KING T.M. FRAZIER

HE EXPECTED ME TO COWER.
HE EXPECTED WRONG.

FIVE STAR WORD SEARCH

d	l	e	n	p	s	e	s	t	u	o	g	x	h	f
x	a	u	p	n	j	k	d	b	n	h	w	e	g	o
n	n	n	f	i	x	t	e	b	p	g	a	a	n	r
y	i	c	g	r	c	a	s	l	u	r	g	x	i	b
a	g	q	b	e	u	j	a	g	t	e	y	l	l	i
d	i	j	x	t	r	c	x	b	d	y	s	s	l	d
h	r	m	i	e	i	o	r	k	o	i	f	s	e	d
d	o	f	k	r	q	e	u	x	w	h	d	g	p	e
u	u	s	y	s	a	f	c	s	n	l	w	t	m	n
l	m	l	l	k	c	i	t	n	a	m	o	r	o	l
q	n	i	i	q	x	i	t	a	b	o	o	o	c	o
k	n	n	a	u	x	r	w	s	l	d	f	u	t	v
y	g	m	f	t	e	a	r	j	e	r	k	e	r	e
g	n	i	l	l	a	r	h	t	n	e	x	g	k	a
z	u	r	q	x	w	i	q	k	h	l	g	w	a	e

WORD LIST:
BEAUTIFUL
COMPELLING
DANGEROUS
ENTHRALLING
EPIC
FORBIDDEN
HEARTBREAKING
LOVE
LYRICAL
ORIGINAL
ROMANTIC
TABOO
TEARJERKER
UNPUTDOWNABLE

DANGEROUS
ROMANCE

"ONE AND A HALF INCHES OF DAMNATION, AND ALL I COULD THINK ABOUT WAS SINKING DEEPER INTO HELL."

PRIEST SIERRA SIMONE

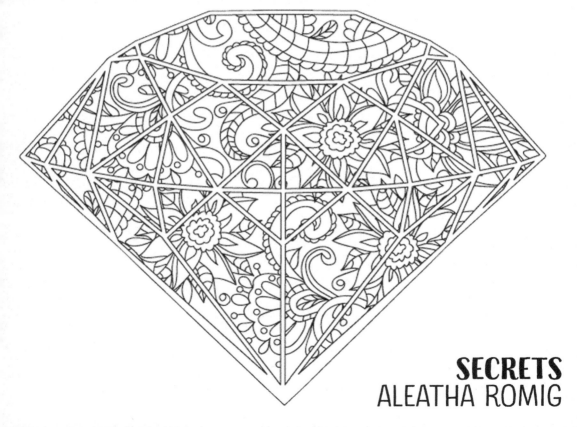

"YOU BELONG TO ME.
YOUR BODY KNOWS IT.
SOON YOUR MIND WILL TOO."

SECRETS
ALEATHA ROMIG

TO-BE-READ LIST MAZE

DIVE INTO THE DEEP END OF YOUR TO-BE-READ LIST TO FIND
OUT WHAT YOU'LL BE READING NEXT.

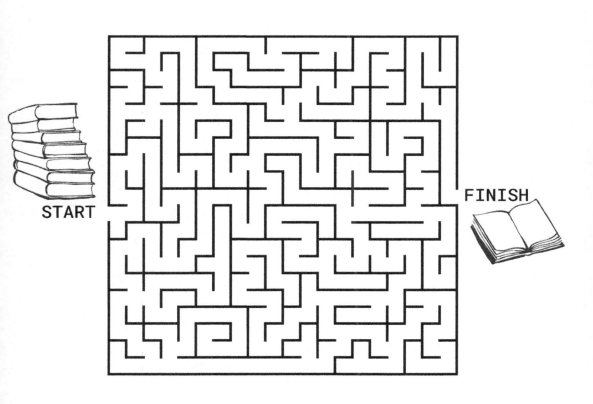

START

FINISH

MERCY
ANNABEL
JOSEPH

"I'M A COLLECTOR
OF BEAUTIFUL THINGS
AND I FIND YOU SO BEAUTIFUL
THAT I HAVE TO HAVE YOU."

HE WAS THE ONE WHO BROKE MY HEART FIRST, AND HERE HE IS AGAIN.

KALEIDOSCOPE HEARTS
CLAIRE CONTRERAS

PARTS OF A BOOK WORD SEARCH

```
f e g o d j j s c y v q n e p
o d e d i c a t i o n p f g r
r t c b f b g n s k a y r a o
m d v s n l o e x r f z j p l
a d r m q o c m a g f j f e o
t k b b c n x g g o n x t l g
t h a e e t r d r u c o m t u
i s y t p a p e u b n m i i e
n r n q p i w l v s r q q t l
g e d h t o l w r t h e e n d
s t s b r e v o c k o o b a y
s p w d o w h n g u o g r v h
n a w p e t s k u u l y r q d
p h a a u c q c a p e r k s c
y c m a w h p a r g i p e m j
```

WORD LIST:
BOOK COVER
EPILOGUE
PROLOGUE
FOREWORD
AUTHOR'S NOTE
ACKNOWLEDGMENTS
EPIGRAPH
DEDICATION
TITLE PAGE
FORMATTING
CHAPTERS
PARAGRAPHS
SENTENCES
THE END

"MAYBE I AM THE MONSTER.
AFTER ALL, I COME OUT
TO PLAY AT NIGHT...
BUT SO DO YOU, LITTLE ONE.
YOU'RE OUT IN THE DARKNESS, TOO."

THE KISS THIEF LJ SHEN

I WANTED HER TO BE MY RELIGION, THE REASON THE SUN ROSE AND FELL EACH DAY.

WELCOME TO THE DARK SIDE GIANA DARLING

HAPPILY EVER AFTER MAZE

FALL IN LOVE, WHERE YOU'LL FIND TURBULENT EMOTIONS AND
SERIOUS CONFLICT ON THE PATH TO THE END.

THE
END

FIRST
SENTENCE

HIS LIPS WERE FRANTIC
AND FRENZIED AGAINST MINE,
AS THOUGH NO MATTER
HOW MUCH I GAVE HIM-
AND I GAVE HIM EVERYTHING
-IT WASN'T ENOUGH.
IT COULD NEVER BE ENOUGH.

DIRTY FILTHY RICH MEN LAURELIN PAIGE

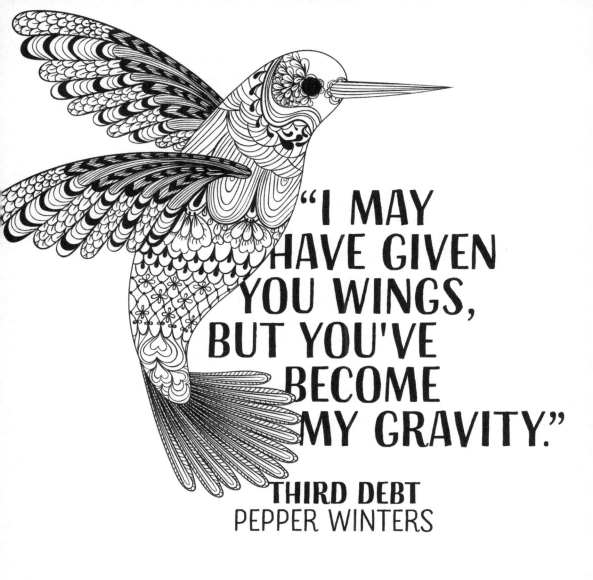

"I MAY HAVE GIVEN YOU WINGS, BUT YOU'VE BECOME MY GRAVITY."

THIRD DEBT
PEPPER WINTERS

"I'D RATHER NOT KILL YOU."

CROW A. ZAVARELLI

I DON'T KNOW HOW TO BEHAVE LIKE A CIVILIZED MAN, BUT I KNOW HOW TO MAKE HER BEG.

SAVAGE MAFIA PRINCE
ANNIKA MARTIN

BOOKSTAGRAM WORD SEARCH

```
k f y m y b f e b g g y r u g
n e c i g l i o g u a s e w a
c o e a a f o v x d z c a h t
s m v t l k g f i a i l d n h
w v l e s y c r r z f e i p s
d a h o l g f u o x a g n s a
y s f x k w d e m d u f g d h
w i b o o k s t a g r a m a y
g p l l e f p e n i b c j e z
s n l h u o r k c r w v j r p
v o f s r a t s e v i f u d f
f v t p t n w f b a a d j o b
w z s s i r e p o s t f w o p
h s n b o o k w o r m o g g p
l i r f u w p e k c i e x s k
```

WORD LIST:

BOOKSTAGRAM
READING
FLATLAY
BOOKSOFIG
ROMANCEBOOK
FIVESTARS
GOODREADS
HASHTAG
REPOST
FOLLOWFRIDAY
BOOKWORM
NOVEL
SHELFIE
INSTAREAD

"I HIRED YOU TO BE
IN CHARGE OF MY CAREER,
BUT YOU'RE NOT ALLOWED
TO MANAGE MY HEART."

SIGNED MARNI MANN

YOU CAN'T EVER LET YOUR GUARD DOW

MERCILESS WILLOW WINTERS

I LIKE YOU COLLARED, BABY.
I LIKE YOU NAKED.
I LIKE YOU MINE.

OWNED M. NEVER

BOOK **MEMORY** MAZE

REMEMBER THAT BOOK WHER SHE... AND THEN HE... AND THEN
WHEN THEY MEET... ENJOY SEARCHING FOR A BOOK WITHOUT
THE TITLE OR AUTHOR NAME!

START LOOKING...

YOU FOUND IT!

HE'S COME TO MAKE GOOD
ON HIS PROMISE...

HE'S BACK TO TAKE THAT
SOMETHING PRECIOUS. ME.

COLLATERAL NATASHA KNIGHT

AUTHOR WORD SEARCH

```
w d k n u s u r g l t b t q w
r o r e d a e r a t e b p i r
y u r s n t l j a s y l i n i
g t b k r o j t t l z c r d t
i u i e i i t n h f f e c i i
h h a v u n u e i v i o s e n
k t b n i o p r b m i l u a g
g v x f c t s r y o d a n u v
e n z d z t a y o r o e a t q
k e r m d o e e l g y k m h q
t o z r c a n e r h r u m o e
w n a i t r f w f c m e j r s
k f g n i t i d e f l i s i u
t i r g d m u g j j o p u s m
r e v i s i n g f v l c p z f
```

WORD LIST:

WRITING
RETREAT
COFFEE
WORD COUNT
FIRST DRAFT
REVISING
EDITING
BETA READER
MUSE
CREATIVITY
WORK IN PROGRESS
MANUSCRIPT
INDIE AUTHOR
NOTEBOOK

MY BRITTLE HEART WOULD NEVER HEAL.

I WAS CONDEMNED TO HIM FOREVER.

DAMIANO DE LUCA
PARKER S. HUNTINGTON

GIANA DARLING CELIA AARON MARNI
MANN NIKKI SLOANE LAURELIN PAIGE
TRISHA WOLFE ALEATHA ROMIG
T.M. FRAZIER CLAIRE CONTRERAS
AUTUMN JONES LAKE M. NEVER
ANNA ZAIRES PARKER S. HUNTINGTON
BB EASTON TESSA BAILEY STYLO
FANTOME R.K. LILLEY B.B. REID
NATASHA KNIGHT ALTA HENSLEY TARA
SUE ME SIERRA SIMONE ANNIKA
MARTIN WILLOW WINTERS A. ZAVARELLI
ANNABEL JOSEPH SHANORA WILLIAMS
PAM GODWIN LI SHEN TAMSEN PARKER

WE VENTURED INTO THE SAME BLACKNESS I COULDN'T SEEM TO ESCAPE, SINKING FURTHER AND FURTHER INTO THE SEA.

AUTHOR SIGNING MAZE

TICKETS, REGISTRATION, WRIST BANDS, OH MY! WORK YOUR WAY THROUGH A HUGE BOOK SIGNING TO SEE YOUR FAVORITE AUTHORS AND GET THEIR SIGNATURES.

START

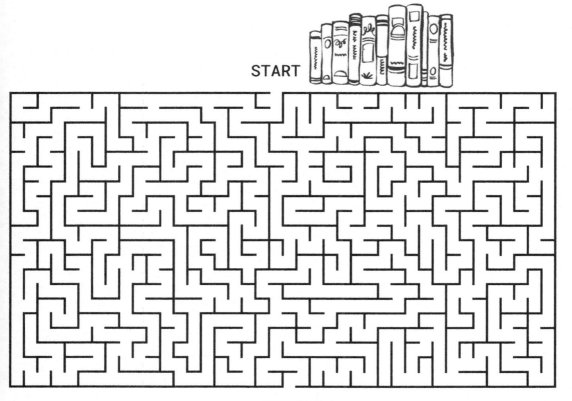

FINISH

HE WAS EVERY BIT AS WILD AS THE FOREST AROUND US

BLACKWOOD
CELIA AARON

"I HAVE NO PROBLEM ADMITTING THAT YOU ARE STILL, TO THIS DAY, PROBABLY THE HOTTEST PUSSY I'VE EVER HAD."

DEGRADATION STYLO FANTOME

"YOU'RE WELCOME IN ADVANCE FOR THE ORGASM."

TOP TROUBLE
TARA SUE ME

BOOK FORMAT WORD SEARCH

```
r f d t c z e x v g b m x k n
y q z t j n a u s i x i s i e
s p e c i a l e d i t i o n w
i u u g o e p k a j g r p d s
k y b j a r m u n f x n x l l
k c m s i p d t k o o b e e e
e k a n c i a n n r q x p d t
r j t b o r e v o c d r a h t
o n u b r d i t i x x e e m e
t t o y e e a p z k b z j u r
s o m f m r p f t n f l o z x
k j d q r y j a l i b r a r y
o e r a q y l t p e o w e h c
o t n g h u r n p o h n o u h
b g k q x g a d m p c s w p p
```

WORD LIST:
PRINT
EBOOK
AUDIOBOOK
NARRATOR
HARDCOVER
PAPERBACK
BOOKSTORE
SUBSCRIPTION
SIGNED
SPECIAL EDITION
LIBRARY
KINDLE
NEWSLETTER
SHELF

HIS TIE WAS THE SAME SHADE OF GREEN AS HIS DADDY'S MONEY

THE INITIATION
NIKKI SLOANE

HIS CUSTODY
TAMSEN PARKER

"I'M GOING TO
TEACH YOU.
AND I'M GOING TO
START HERE."

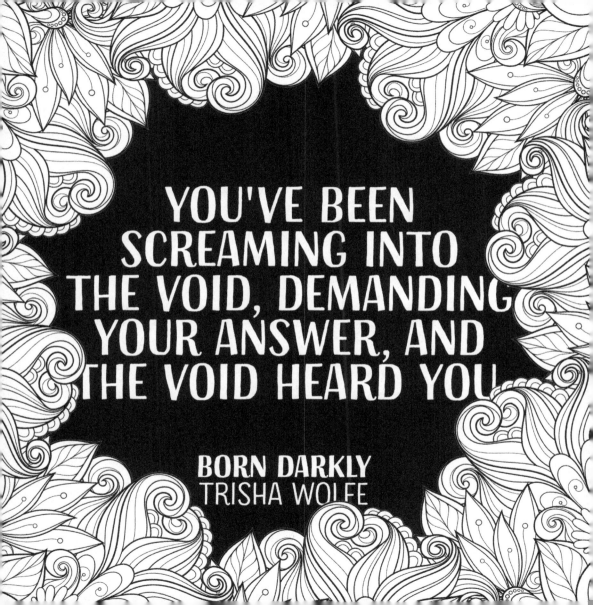

READ ME ROMANCE MAZE

THE READ ME ROMANCE PODCAST HAS ORIGINAL AUDIOBOOKS FOR FREE. MATCH THE TITLE TO THE AUTHOR!

TESSA BAILEY

SKYE WARREN

SIERRA SIMONE

HEAVY EQUIP-MENT

RENAI-SSANCE MAN

AN AMERICAN SQUIRE

SHE FEELS LIKE HEAVEN-
WARMTH AND
GOODNESS
AND EVERY HOME
I NEVER HAD.

HOSTAGE SKYE WARREN AND ANNIKA MARTIN

WE HOPE YOU LOVED OUR COLORING PAGES! KEEP READING TO LEARN MORE ABOUT THE BOOKS FEATURED IN THE COLLECTION.

TWIST ME BY ANNA ZAIRES

A man obsessed. A girl abducted. The darkest love story ever told…

Kidnapped. Taken to a private island.

I never thought this could happen to me. I never imagined one chance meeting on the eve of my eighteenth birthday could change my life so completely.

Now I belong to him. To Julian. To a man who is as ruthless as he is beautiful—a man whose touch makes me burn. A man whose tenderness I find more devastating than his cruelty.

My captor is an enigma. I don't know who he is or why he took me. There is a darkness inside him—a darkness that scares me even as it draws me in.

My name is Nora Leston, and this is my story.

LEARN MORE AT: WWW.ANNAZAIRES.COM

THE PAWN BY SKYE WARREN

The price of survival…

Gabriel Miller swept into my life like a storm. He tore down my father with cold retribution, leaving him penniless in a hospital bed. I quit my private all-girl's college to take care of the only family I have left.

There's one way to save our house, one thing I have left of value.

My virginity.

A forbidden auction…

Gabriel appears at every turn. He seems to take pleasure in watching me fall. Other times he's the only kindness in a brutal underworld.

Except he's playing a deeper game than I know. Every move brings us together, every secret rips us apart. And when the final piece is played, only one of us can be left standing.

LEARN MORE AT: WWW.SKYEWARREN.COM

KING BY T.M. FRAZIER

Homeless. Hungry. Desperate. Doe has no memories of who she is or where she comes from. A notorious career criminal just released from prison, King is someone you don't want to cross unless you're prepared to pay him back in blood, sweat, sex, or a combination of all three. King's future hangs in the balance. Doe's is written in her past. When they come crashing together, they will have to learn that sometimes in order to hold on, you have to first let go.

LEARN MORE AT: WWW.TMFRAZIERBOOKS.COM

FEAR ME BY B.B. REID

This isn't another *"I hate you because I secretly love you"* story. Boy really does hate girl.

I don't believe in fairy tales and Prince Charming.

I believe in fear.

He taught me how to be afraid.

We first met on a playground on a wonderful summer day. It was the first time he hurt me and it wouldn't be the last. For ten years, he's been my tormentor and I've been his forbidden. But then he went away, and yet I was still afraid.

Now he's back and wants more than just my tears. You see…he thinks I sent him away so now he wants revenge…and he knows just how to get it.

LEARN MORE AT: WWW.BBREID.COM

PRIEST BY SIERRA SIMONE

There are many rules a priest can't break. A priest cannot marry. A priest cannot abandon his flock. A priest cannot forsake his God.

I've always been good at following rules.

Until she came. Then I learned new rules.

My name is Tyler Anselm Bell. I'm twenty-nine years old. Six months ago, I broke my vow of celibacy on the altar of my own church, and God help me, I would do it again.

I am a priest and this is my confession.

LEARN MORE AT: WWW.THESIERRASIMONE.COM

SECRETS BY ALEATHA ROMIG

I'm Sterling Sparrow. You've no doubt heard my name or read it on the top of tall buildings. There's more to my business—my realm—than what is seen aboveground.

Within the underbelly of one of America's largest cities lives a world where a man's word is either his most valuable tool or his most respected weapon. When my father ruled that world and that city, he promised me someone who would one day make my reign complete.

Since that day, long ago, Araneae McCrie has been mine.

She just didn't know.

My father is now gone.

The city and the underbelly are now mine.

The time has come for me to collect who was promised to me, to shred her life of secrets and make her who she's always been—mine.

LEARN MORE AT: WWW.ALEATHAROMIG.COM

MERCY BY ANNABEL JOSEPH

Lucy Merritt has always defined herself by her body, whether dancing in a small avant-garde company or posing for art. But she has always felt as if something is wrong with her, as if something is missing. She has never been in love.

Suddenly, in the darkness of the theater wings, a strangely affecting man enters her life. Matthew Norris, rich, handsome patron of the dance company, has decided that he wants Lucy for his own. He makes her an offer that both frightens and compels her, and they soon begin an affair characterized by only two requirements, beauty and truth.

But how truthful are Matthew and Lucy? How much of Matthew's strenuous brand of love can Lucy endure? And how long can their rigid Dom/sub relationship stay frozen in time, never growing, never moving forward?

LEARN MORE AT: WWW.ANNABELJOSEPH.COM

DARK NOTES BY PAM GODWIN

They call me a slut. Maybe I am.

Sometimes I do things I despise.

Sometimes men take without asking.

But I have a musical gift, only a year left of high school, and a plan.

With one obstacle.

Emeric Marceaux doesn't just take.

He seizes my will power and bangs it like a dark note.

When he commands me to play, I want to give him everything.

I kneel for his punishments, tremble for his touch, and risk it all for our stolen moments.

He's my obsession, my master, my music.

And my teacher.

LEARN MORE AT: WWW.PAMGODWIN.COM

SKIN BY BB EASTON

In 1997, Ronald "Knight" McKnight was the meanest, most misunderstood boy at Peach State High School … perhaps on the entire planet. Knight hated everyone, except for me, BB—the perky, quirky punk chick with the locker next to his.

I, on the other hand, liked everybody … except for Knight. I was scared sh*tless of him, actually. All I wanted was to marry Prince Eric-lookalike and king of the Peach State High punk scene, Lance Hightower, and have a million of his babies.

Unfortunately for me, Knight was even better at getting his way than I was, and once he got under my skin, my life would never be the same.

LEARN MORE AT: WWW.ARTBYEASTON.COM

KALEIDOSCOPE HEARTS BY CLAIRE CONTRERAS

He was my older brother's best friend.

He was never supposed to be mine.

I thought we would get it out of our system and move on.

One of us did.

One of us left.

Now he's back, looking at me like he wants to devour me. And all those feelings I'd turned into anger are brewing into something else, something that terrifies me.

He broke my heart last time.

This time he'll obliterate it.

LEARN MORE AT: WWW.CLAIRECONTRERASBOOKS.COM

THE KISS THIEF BY LJ SHEN

They say your first kiss should be earned.

Mine was stolen by a devil in a masquerade mask under the black Chicago sky.

They say the vows you take on your wedding day are sacred.

Mine were broken before we left church.

They say your heart only beats for one man.

Mine split and bled for two rivals who fought for it until the bitter end.

I was promised to Angelo Bandini, the heir to one of the most powerful families in the Chicago Outfit. Then taken by Senator Wolfe Keaton, who held my father's sins over his head to force me into marriage.

They say that all great love stories have a happy ending.

I, Francesca Rossi, found myself erasing and rewriting mine until the very last chapter.

One kiss.

Two men.

Three lives.

Entwined together.

And somewhere between these two men, I had to find my forever.

LEARN MORE AT: WWW.AUTHORLJSHEN.COM

IN FLIGHT BY R.K. LILLEY

When reserved flight attendant Bianca gets one look at billionaire hotel owner James Cavendish, she loses all of her hard-won composure. For a girl who can easily juggle a tray of champagne flutes at 35,000 feet in three inch heels, she finds herself shockingly weak-kneed from their first encounter. The normally unruffled Bianca can't seem to look away from his electrifying turquoise gaze. They hold a challenge, and a promise, that she finds impossible to resist, and she is a girl who is used to saying no and meaning it.

Bianca is accustomed to dealing with super-models and movie stars in her job as a first class flight attendant, but James Cavendish puts them all to shame in the looks department. If only it were just his looks that she found so irresistible about the intimidating man, Bianca could have ignored his attentions. But what tempts her like never before is the dominant pull he seems to have over her from the moment they meet, and the promise of pleasure, and pain, that she reads in his eyes.

LEARN MORE AT: WWW.RKLILLEY.COM

WELCOME TO THE DARK SIDE
BY GIANA DARLING

I was a good girl.

I ate my vegetables, volunteered at the local autism centre and sat in the front pew of church every Sunday.

Then, I got cancer.

What the hell kind of reward was that for a boring life well lived?

I was a seventeen-year-old paradigm of virtue and I was tired of it.

So, when I finally ran into the man I'd been writing to since he saved my life as a little girl and he offered to show me the dark side of life before I left it for good, I said yes.

Only, I didn't know that Zeus Garro was the President of The Fallen MC and when you made a deal with a man who is worse than the devil, there was no going back...

LEARN MORE AT: WWW.GIANADARLING.COM

DIRTY FILTHY RICH MEN
BY LAURELIN PAIGE

When I met Donovan Kincaid, I knew he was rich. I didn't know he was filthy. Truth be told, I was only trying to get his best friend to notice me.

I knew poor scholarship girls like me didn't stand a chance against guys like Weston King and Donovan Kincaid, but I was in love with his world, their world, of parties and sex and power. I knew what I wanted—I knew who I wanted—until one night, their world tried to bite me back and Donovan saved me. He saved me, and then Weston finally noticed me, and I finally learned what it was to be in their world.

And then what it was like to lose it.

Ten years later, I've found my way back. Back to their world. Back to him.

This time, I'm ready. I've been down this road before, and I know all the dirty, filthy ways Donovan will try and wreck me.

But it's hard to resist. Especially when I know how much I'll like it.

LEARN MORE AT: WWW.LAURELINPAIGE.COM

THIRD DEBT BY PEPPER WINTERS

"She healed me. She broke me. I set her free. But we are in this together. We will end this together. The rules of this ancient game can't be broken."

Nila Weaver no longer recognises herself. She's left her lover, her courage, and her promise. Two debts down. Too many to go.

Jethro Hawk no longer recognises himself. He's embraced what he always ran from, and now faces punishment far greater than he feared.

It's almost time. It's demanding to be paid.

The Third Debt will be the ultimate test…

LEARN MORE AT: WWW.PEPPERWINTERS.COM

CROW BY A. ZAVARELLI

He's a killer. A mobster.

The last man on earth I'd ever want to be with. I won't lose my head just because he's hot, Irish, and has a wicked accent to boot.

He's one of the only leads in my best friend's disappearance, and I don't trust him.

So I've got a few rules in mind when it comes to dealing with Lachlan Crow.

1. Keep a clear head and don't get distracted.

2. Do what's necessary and never forget why you're there.

3. Never, and I mean never, fall for him.

Fourth and final rule?

Throw out the book altogether. Because the rules don't apply when it comes to the Irish mafia.

It was only supposed to be temporary, but now Lachlan thinks he owns me. He says he's not letting me go.

And I believe him.

LEARN MORE AT: WWW.AZAVARELLI.COM

SAVAGE MAFIA PRINCE
BY ANNIKA MARTIN

Where is Kiro?

He's the lost Dragusha brother, heir to a vast mafia empire—brilliant, violent, and utterly savage… and he's been missing for years.

ANN

I'm supposed to be doing simple undercover research at the Fancher Institute for the Mentally Ill & Dangerous, but I can't keep my mind off Patient 34. He's startlingly young and gorgeous, but it's not just that. He's strapped way too tightly to that bed. And there's no name or criminal history on his chart. What are these people hiding? My reporter's instincts are screaming. Here's the other thing: the staffers here believe he's so sedated that there's not a thought in his head, but I catch him watching me when nobody's looking. Our connection sizzles when I enter the room. When our eyes meet, I know he understands me in a way nobody else ever has. I'm supposed to follow my editor's orders—I have secrets, too—but everything about Patient 34 is suspicious. How can I not investigate?

LEARN MORE AT:
WWW.ANNIKAMARTINBOOKS.COM

SIGNED BY MARNI MANN

A one-night stand with James Ryne, the hottest actress in LA, was a night I'd never forget…

James: I can't stop thinking about you.

Brett: I didn't know America's sweetheart was such a dirty girl.

James: It gets better.

Brett: You're too young for me.

James: Eighteen's the age of consent.

Brett: The things I want to do to you right now…

James: Are you ever going to tell me who you really are?

Brett: The best you've ever had. That's all you need to know.

James: When are you coming back to LA?

Brett: Next week—and you'd better not be wearing panties.

Brett: What the hell did I just watch?

James: Oh my God, Brett! It's going viral!

James: My life is ruined. My career. My reputation.

James: Are you there?

James: Will you let me explain?

James: Brett?

Brett: Forget everything I said before. Forget us.

I tried to forget her…until she walked into my office, begging to get signed.

LEARN MORE AT: WWW.MARNISMANN.COM

MERCILESS BY WILLOW WINTERS

I should've known she would ruin me the moment I saw her.

Women like her are made to destroy men like me.

I couldn't resist her though.

Given to me to start a war; I was too eager to accept.

But I didn't know what she'd do to me. That she would change everything.

She sees through me in a way no one else ever has.

Her innocence and vulnerability make me weak for her and I hate it.

I know better than to give in to temptation.

A ruthless man doesn't let a soul close to him.

A cold-hearted man doesn't risk anything for anyone.

A powerful man with a beautiful woman at his mercy … he doesn't fall for her.

LEARN MORE AT:
WWW.WILLOWWINTERSWRITES.COM

OWNED BY M. NEVER

Ellie Stevens has lusted over Kayne Roberts since he first walked into the import/export company she works for a little over a year ago. As Expo's most important client, Ellie has always kept a safe distance from the man with the majestic blue eyes—until temptation finally gets the better of her. Impulsively, Ellie invites Kayne to one of Expo's infamous company parties her flamboyant boss is notorious for throwing. Unbeknownst to Ellie, the god in the Armani suit isn't just the suave entrepreneur he portrays himself to be. Underneath the professional exterior is a man with a secret life, dark desires, and nefarious contacts.

In a hidden corner of a trendy New York City lounge, the spark kindling between the two of them ignites. Unable to resist the sinful attraction, Ellie agrees to leave with Kayne, believing she is finally bedding the man of her dreams. Little does she know when she walks out the door, she's about to be Owned.

LEARN MORE AT: WWW.MNEVERAUTHOR.COM

COLLATERAL BY NATASHA KNIGHT

Stefan Sabbioni showed up in my bedroom on my sixteenth birthday. Uninvited, he stood in the shadows smelling of whiskey and death and wrapped a broken, blood-crusted necklace around my neck.

I thought he'd strangle me with it.

That night, he left a message for my father. He said he'd be back to take something precious.

I never delivered that message, though. I wonder if things would be different if I had because now, two years later, he's back. And he's not hiding in any shadows.

He's come to make good on his promise.

He's back to take that something precious.

Me.

LEARN MORE AT: WWW.NATASHA-KNIGHT.COM

ROUGH RHYTHM BY TESSA BAILEY

God help the woman I take home tonight.

Band manager James Brandon never expected to find the elusive satisfaction he'd been chasing, let alone stumble upon it in some sleezy Hollywood meat market. Yet the girl's quiet pride spoke to him from across the bar, louder than a shout. Troubled, hungry and homeless, she'd placed her trust in him. But after losing the grip on his dark desires that one fateful night, James has spent the last four years atoning for letting her down.

This time I'll finally crack him.

Rock band drummer Lita Regina has had enough of James's guilt. She wants the explosive man she met that night in Hollywood. The man who held nothing back and took no prisoners—save Lita. And she'll stop at nothing to revive him. Even if it means throwing herself into peril at every turn, just to get a reaction from her stoic manager. But when Lita takes her quest one step too far, James disappears from her life, thinking his absence will keep her safe.

Now it's up to Lita to bring James back…and ignite an inferno of passion in the process.

LEARN MORE AT: WWW.TESSABAILEY.COM

SLOW BURN
BY AUTUMN JONES LAKE

I'm not used to women who say no to me.

As president of the Lost Kings MC, women are always eager to jump in my bed.

Not Hope.

She's a lawyer.

I'm an outlaw.

She's strong-willed and smart-mouthed.

I ruthlessly protect what's mine.

Hope Kendal is mine. Even if she doesn't know it yet.

We have nothing in common.

We're not meant to be.

Or are we?

LEARN MORE AT: WWW.AUTUMNJONESLAKE.COM

DAMIANO DE LUCA BY
PARKER S. HUNTINGTON

Ten years ago, I crushed Damiano De Luca's heart, vowing false promises I never delivered.

The revenge? Didn't happen.

The destruction? As if I could.

Betrayal? Not. A. Chance.

We were 18 when I left, taking my secrets with me.

Now at 28, there's no trace of the jaded mafia prince with the protective streak.

He's crueler. Colder. More calculated than ever.

And he's glaring at me from a funeral pew, looking at me and my wedding ring like we should be the ones buried six feet under.

The war is back on, but I'm not that teenaged girl anymore.

This time, there will be blood.

And it won't be mine.

**LEARN MORE AT:
WWW.PARKERSHUNTINGTON.COM**

BASTARDS & WHISKEY
BY ALTA HENSELY

I sit amongst the Presidents, Royalty, the Captains of Industry, and the wealthiest men in the world.

We own Spiked Roses—an exclusive, membership only establishment in New Orleans where money or lineage is the only way in. It is for the gentlemen who own everything and never hear the word no.

Sipping on whiskey, smoking cigars, and conducting multi-million dollar deals in our own personal playground of indulgence, there isn't anything I can't have… and that includes HER. I can also have HER if I want.

And I want.

LEARN MORE AT: WWW.ALTAHENSLEY.COM

TAINTED BLACK
BY SHANORA WILLIAMS

Dear Mr. Black,

I know you were hurting. I heard your cries. I wished over and over again that I could make it better, but as you stated I was too inexperienced; too good for someone as bad as you.

Perhaps you were right, but it didn't matter because what I did know was that I loved the way you felt—loved the way you smelled. I loved how hard you got for me, and when you called me your Little Knight.

I can still remember that day in the park, when you held me close and kissed me deep. How you effortlessly made me cry your name on top of sweet-smelling grass, making me feel like the only girl in the world. I loved how you looked at me, how you spoke to me.

I had been madly in love with you ever since I was twelve years old, but I shouldn't have been.

Isabelle would have hated it—my best friend. I couldn't afford to lose her. Besides, you two had already lost enough. Losing Mrs. Black was the epitome.

It's Chloe Knight.

I wanted to be there for you no matter what, but Isabelle needed me too.

And she would have hated me if she ever found out I was sleeping with her father.

LEARN MORE AT: WWW.SHANORAWILLIAMS.COM

BLACKWOOD BY CELIA AARON

I dig. It's what I do. I'll literally use a shovel to answer a question. Some answers, though, have been buried too deep for too long. But I'll find those, too. And I know where to dig—the Blackwood Estate on the edge of the Mississippi Delta. Garrett Blackwood is the only thing standing between me and the truth. A broken man—one with desires that dance in the darkest part of my soul—he's either my savior or my enemy. I'll dig until I find all his secrets. Then I'll run so he never finds mine. The only problem? He likes it when I run.

LEARN MORE AT: WWW.CELIAAARON.COM

DEGRADATION BY STYLO FANTOME

Eighteen year old Tatum O'Shea is a naive, shy, little rich girl. Twenty-three year old Jameson Kane is smart, seductive, and richer. They come together for one night, one explosion, one mistake, and Tate is hurled into space—no family, no money, and no Jameson.

Seven years later, life is going pretty good for Tate, when she runs into Jameson again. This time, she thinks she's ready for him. She doesn't have a naive bone left in her body, and she can't even remember what shy feels like. Jameson has evolved, as well—sharp words, sharper wit, and a tongue that can cut her in half. It all sounds like fun to a woman like Tate, and she is ready to play, determined to prove that she isn't the same girl he conquered once before. A series of games start, each one more devious than the last.

But as the line between games and reality becomes blurry, Tate quickly learns that Jameson has most definitely earned his nickname, "Satan". Can she beat him at his own game before someone gets hurt? Or will he leave her soulless, making him the winner, once and for all?

LEARN MORE AT:
WWW.AMAZON.COM/AUTHOR/STYLOFANTOME

TOP TROUBLE BY TARA SUE ME

Some say they've been arguing for years.

Others say it's just a really long foreplay session.

When Kelly moves from Wilmington, Delaware to Dallas, Texas, Evan regrets all the time they spent arguing and knows he made a mistake in letting her go. A wedding allows them the opportunity to reconnect and they spend a passionate night together. Yet when morning comes Kelly seems further away than ever.

Kelly has her reasons for treating Evan the way she did, not to mention a secret or two she's never shared with anyone. If she hurt Evan, she's sorry but she had no other choice. Besides, they're both Tops, and they'd never be right together.

An unexpected situation forces them back together, and for a couple who's done little else than bicker, the danger they find themselves in might be what they need to finally admit how they feel for each other.

Or it might be what pulls them apart forever.

LEARN MORE AT: WWW.TARASUEME.COM

THE INITIATION BY NIKKI SLOANE

No one knows how new members are selected to the board of Hale Banking and Holding. But there are rumors of a sordid rite of initiation.

Whispers how one woman and nine men disappear into a boardroom.

This time, that woman will be me.

The Hale family owns everything—the eighth largest bank in the world, everyone in our town, even the mortgage on my parents' mansion. And now Royce Hale wants to own me.

He is charming. Seductive. Ruthless. But above all, he's the prince of lies. My body may tighten with white-hot desire under his penetrating gaze, but I refuse to enjoy it.

I'll make a deal with the devil to save my family and sell myself to the Hales. But Royce will never own my heart.

LEARN MORE AT: WWW.NIKKISLOANE.COM

HIS CUSTODY BY TAMSEN PARKER

He needs to be a better man for her sake, but she makes him want to be so bad…

Keyne O'Connell leads a charmed life. She has a caring family and a terrific boyfriend. Her senior year is about to begin, and her future looks bright. But one dark summer night robs her of everyone she loves, thrusting her into the care of her boyfriend's intimidating, much older brother.

Dark and brooding, Jasper Andersson is not a good man. His business dealings are barely legal. He's a womanizer and a casual drug user. He has no interest in becoming Keyne's guardian, although given her limited options, he doesn't have much of a choice. He knows he must protect her at whatever the cost.

But living in close quarters soon stirs up feelings inside them both that are far from platonic. Keyne needs a firm hand to keep her in line, but what she desires could lead Jasper into trouble…

LEARN MORE AT: WWW.TAMSENPARKER.COM

BORN DARKLY BY TRISHA WOLFE

He challenged her sanity.

She shattered his reality.

They dared each other…to the brink of madness.

A dark and twisted maze awaits criminal psychologist London Noble when she falls for her patient, convicted serial killer, Grayson Pierce Sullivan. As she unravels the traps, her sanity tested with each game, she's forced to acknowledge the true evil in the world around her.

LEARN MORE AT WWW.TRISHAWOLFE.COM

HOSTAGE
BY SKYE WARREN & ANNIKA MARTIN

I'd never even kissed a boy the night I met Stone. The night I saw him kill. The night he spared my life. That was only the beginning.

He turns up in my car again and again, dangerous and full of raw power. "Drive," he tells me, and I have no choice. He's a criminal with burning green eyes, invading my life and my dreams.

The police say he's dangerously obsessed with me, but I'm the one who can't stop thinking about him. Maybe it's wrong to let him touch me. Maybe it's wrong to touch him back. Maybe these twisted dates need to stop. Except he feels like the only real thing in my world of designer labels and mansions.

So I drive us under threat, until it's hard to remember I don't want to be there.

Until it's too late to turn back.

LEARN MORE AT: WWW.SKYEWARREN.COM
& WWW.ANNIKAMARTINBOOKS.COM

Made in the USA
Columbia, SC
30 January 2020

87270224R00083